OLD MOTHER HUBBARD
AND HER WONDERFUL DOG

ILLUSTRATED BY

JAMES MARSHALL

A SUNBURST BOOK

FARRAR, STRAUS AND GIROUX

Old Mother Hubbard
Went to the cupboard,
To fetch her poor dog a bone;

But when she came there
The cupboard was bare
And so the poor dog had none.

She went to the baker
To buy him some bread;

But when she came back
The poor dog was dead.

She went to the undertaker
To buy him a coffin;

But when she came back
The poor dog was laughing.

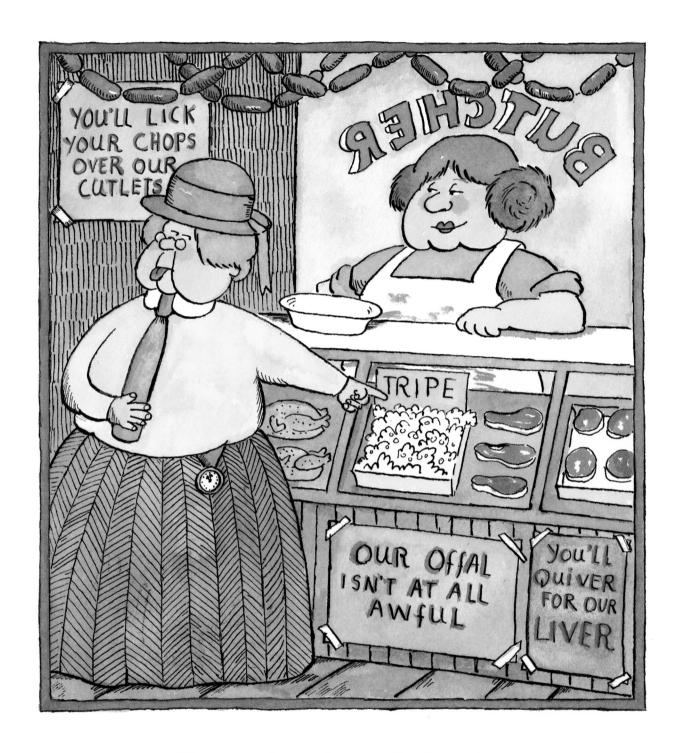

She took a clean dish
To get him some tripe;

But when she came back
He was smoking a pipe.

She went to the fishmonger
To buy him some fish;

But when she came back
He was licking his dish.

But when she came back
The dog stood on his head.

She went to the fruit stand
To buy him some fruit;

But when she came back
He was playing the flute.

She went to the tailor
To buy him a coat;

But when she came back
He was riding a goat.

She went to the hatter
To buy him a hat;

But when she got back
He was feeding the cat.

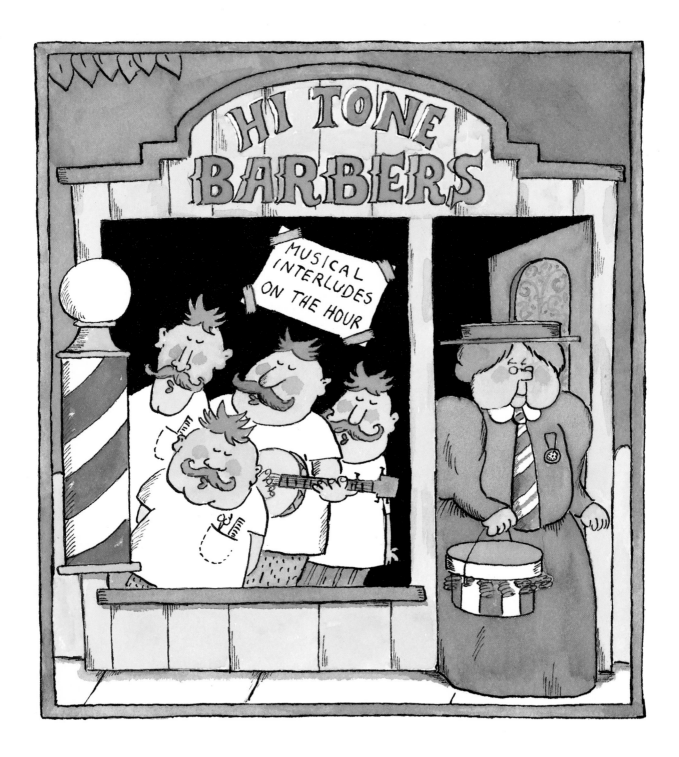

She went to the barber
To buy him a wig;

She went to the cobbler
To buy him some shoes;

But when she came back
   He was reading the news.

She went to the seamstress
To buy him some linen;

But when she came back
    The dog was a-spinning.

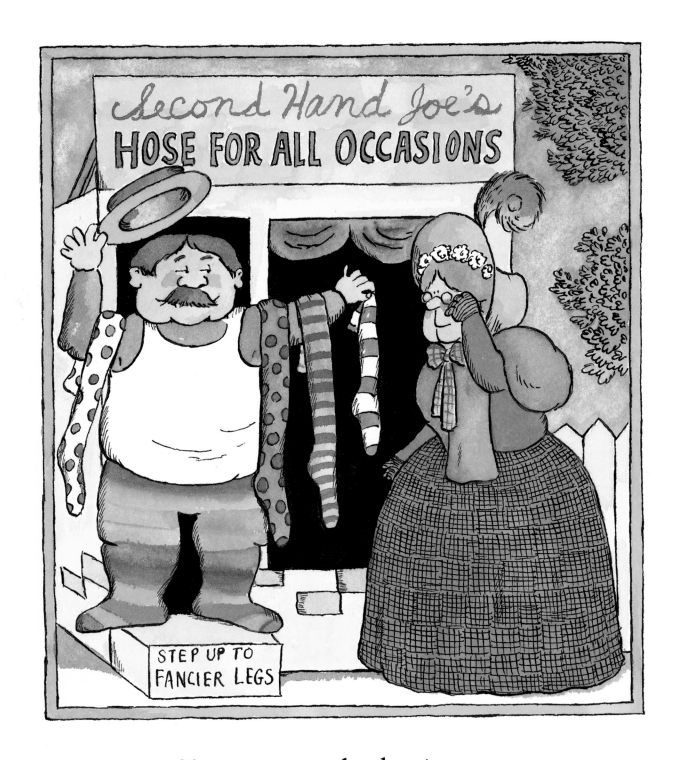

She went to the hosier
To buy him some hose;

But when she came back

He was dressed in his clothes.
The dame made a curtsey,
The dog made a bow;

The dame said, Your servant,
The dog said:

For Michael di Capua